LITTLE MOUSE'S PAINTING

LITTLE MOUSE'S PAINTING

Diane Wolkstein
pictures by Maryjane Begin

SeaStar Books

NEW YORK

For Rebekah Wolkstein
D.W.

To my grandmother, Mary Jane
M.B.

Text © 1992 by Diane Wolkstein
Illustrations © 1992 by Maryjane Begin
Music and text © 1990 by Shirley Keller
First published in 1992 by William Morrow and Company, New York.

SEASTAR BOOKS
A division of NORTH-SOUTH BOOKS INC.

Published in the United States by SeaStar Books,
a division of North-South Books Inc., New York.
Published simultaneously in Great Britain, Canada, Australia, and New Zealand
by North-South Books, an imprint of Nord-Süd Verlag AG, Gossau Zürich, Switzerland.

Library of Congress Cataloging-in-Publication Data is available.
A CIP catalogue record for this book is available from The British Library.
The artwork for this book was prepared by using watercolor
and acrylic paints on D'arches watercolor paper.

ISBN 1-58717-124-4 (reinforced trade edition)
1 3 5 7 9 RTE 10 8 6 4 2
ISBN 1-58717-125-2 (paperback edition)
1 3 5 7 9 PB 10 8 6 4 2

Printed in Hong Kong

For more information about our books, and the authors and artists who create them,
visit our web site: www.northsouth.com

Little Mouse's Painting

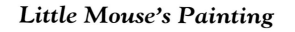

I   see a   flo-wer,   you   see a   tree.

I   see   you   and   you   see   me.

We   see   what   we   want   to   see,

In   Lit-tle   Mou-se's   paint - ing.

Little Mouse lived in her own pretty house under the earth. She had a sweet-smelling bed made of pinewood and honeysuckle vines, a small braided rug, and a painting by her grandmother that hung on the wall over her cupboard. Every day Little Mouse ate her breakfast of berries and nuts, made her bed, and went up the steps to visit her friends.

Bear, Squirrel, and Porcupine were Little Mouse's friends. Some days she picked berries and nuts with Bear. "HO-HO!" Bear would shout whenever he found a particularly fine patch of berries. "Ahhh...AHHH..." he would sigh as he happily ate them.

Some days Little Mouse was invited to Squirrel's tree house, where they had tea and crackers and flowers. Squirrel loved flowers. Sometimes he arranged them carefully in acorn cups, and sometimes he ate them.

Other days Little Mouse went for long walks with Porcupine. Porcupine never walked in a straight line but wandered from one side of the path to the other. She'd often stop to look at something closely and say, "Oh, look at that stone—just look at that stone." Or, "Look at that cloud—just look at that cloud." Then Little Mouse would also pause and examine the stone or quietly stare at the cloud.

But one evening, even though she liked to see her friends, Little Mouse decided she would do something by herself. She decided she would make a painting.

The next morning Little Mouse set up her grandmother's easel near a blueberry bush and began to paint. The sun shone on her.

She made long thin strokes.

She made short thick strokes.

She painted all morning, singing as she worked, and only stopped from time to time for a snack of berries. By afternoon her painting was finished.

As she was looking at it, she heard *thump . . . thump . . . thump.*

It was Bear. Little Mouse hid behind a tree.

"HO-HO!" cried Bear. "That's a beautiful painting. A bear must have painted that painting."

"*No!*" cried Little Mouse, coming out from behind the tree. "I did."

"*You?*" asked Bear, surprised.

"Yes, me."

"Well, I like the bear in the middle of the painting."

"It's not a bear. It's a blueberry bush."

"It's a bear!"

"It's a blueberry bush!"

"Where?" cried Squirrel from his tree. Squirrel looked from Bear to the painting and said, "What bear? What berry? That's a squirrel."

"Where? What squirrel?" cried Bear and Little Mouse together.

Squirrel pointed to the bottom of the painting.

"No!" said Little Mouse, shaking her head. "That's a daisy."

"A daisy? That's a squirrel!"

"It's a daisy!"

"STOP!" shouted Bear. "Let's go see Porcupine. She's sure to know."

Bear thumped along carrying the easel. Squirrel raced ahead with the paintbrushes. And Little Mouse went the slowest, for she was holding the painting.

When they arrived at Porcupine's house, Bear called, "Porcupine, please come out. We have something important to show you."

Porcupine came out of her house and saw Bear, Squirrel, and Little Mouse staring at a painting, which they had placed under an elm tree. She stared, too. Then she said, "Look at the porcupine—just look at that porcupine!"

"What porcupine? Where?" cried Squirrel, Bear, and Little Mouse.

"There—" Porcupine said, pointing to the top of the painting.

"No! No!" the others shouted.

"That's a bear!"

"That's a squirrel!"

"No, *no!*" Little Mouse cried. But no one paid any attention to her. So she said to the elm, "Perhaps *you* would like to know what I think? Yes, good, then I'll tell you. The sun is at the top. The blueberry bush is in the middle, and the daisy with the leaf is at the bottom.

"I know. How do I know? I know because I painted it!"

"Well, now," said Porcupine. "I think I'll take a closer look." Porcupine went up very close to the painting. "Look!" she cried.

Squirrel went up very close to the painting. "A flower *and* a leaf. How yummy!" he said.

Then Bear went up to the painting. "HO-HO!" he shouted. "The blueberry bush. I see the blueberry bush. From close up I can see the blueberry bush!"

"And I can see the sun's rays!" cried Porcupine. "Do you know, I think the blueberry bush looks a lot like you, Bear."

"Hummm," sighed Bear, quite pleased.

"It's a beautiful painting," said Squirrel.

"Leave it here for us to look at," said Porcupine.

Little Mouse left her painting on the easel all day. But when the stars came out, she rolled it up, picked up her grandmother's easel, and carried the painting and the easel and the paintbrushes to her house.

Little Mouse hung the painting on the wall opposite her bed. She sat on her bed and looked at the painting. She walked around her room and looked at it from many different places. She sat on her rug. She jumped up onto her cupboard. She sat on her bed again.

Then she said, "Bear is right. When I sit on my bed far from the painting, the blueberry bush looks like Bear; but when I am very close to the painting, the blueberry bush looks just like the blueberry bush."

Little Mouse ate her supper of berries and nuts. She drank a glass of water and tucked herself into bed.

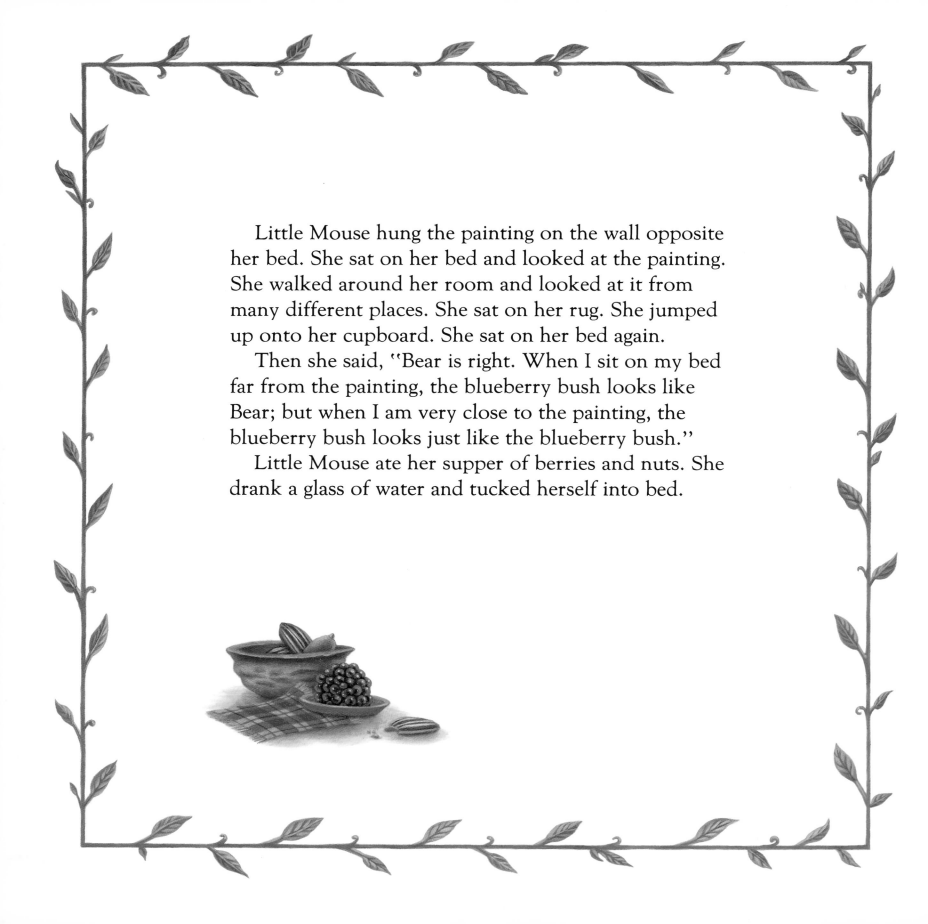

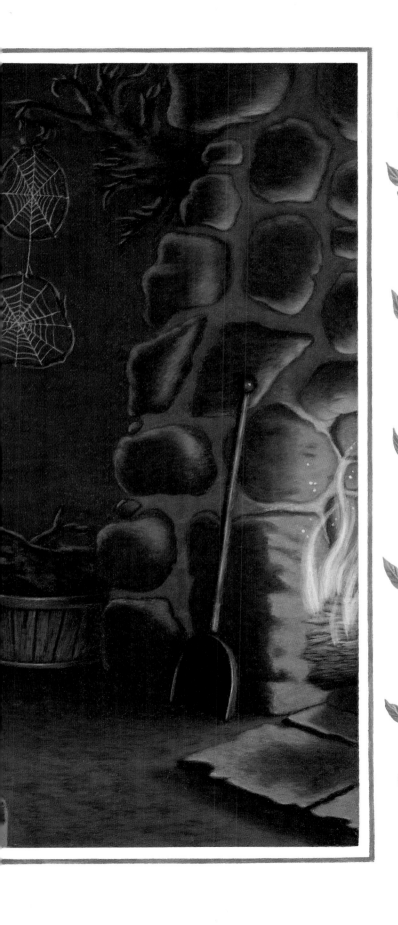

From her bed, she
looked at her painting of
Bear, Squirrel, and Porcupine.
Then she closed her eyes,
smiled happily, and said,
"Good night, Squirrel.
Good night, Porcupine.
Good night, Bear. Good
night, my friends. I'm glad
you're all in my painting."
And Little Mouse fell asleep.

Soon she began to dream.

And in her dream she saw clouds, trees, and stones, all of which looked a little like Bear, Squirrel, Porcupine, and Little Mouse.